This book belongs to

....

ISBN 978-1-64638-330-6

www.cottagedoorpress.com

I Spy with My Little Eye

CHRISTMAS
JINGLE & FIND

cottage door press

Written by Holly Berry-Byrd
Illustrated by Katya Longhi

It was Christmas Eve

I spy with my little eye
4 things that start with M:
a motorcycle, moose,
mop, and mountain.

MAIL

WRAP CENTER

Can you spot
2 polar bears?

SANTA'S HOUSE

Can you find a special house
in this big scene? It has
3 windows and a chimney,
but the door isn't green.

at the busy North Pole...

Look up and down these busy lanes.
Can you find a door made of candy canes?

NORTH POLE KNITTING CIRCLE

NORTH POLE PADDOCK

TOY FACTORY

CAFE

This is Santa's busiest time of year.
Can you find him in every scene?

It would be tasty and quite dandy to find a rainbow of canes made from candy.

NORTH POLE PADDOCK

CANDY Co.

...And the reindeer were missing! Where did they go?

REINDEER WRANGLER

Count 7 red birds.

There's lots of hoofprints on the ground, but whose pawprints are these all around?

I spy with my little eye 5 things that start with T: a teapot, truck, table, top hat, and tree.

Hungry Dasher stopped by

Hot cocoa is an elf's favorite drink. Where is the mug with one snowflake that's pink?

the lunchroom for a bite.

Find 2 purple hats.

SUGAR

FLOUR

These fast, busy elves make baking fun, but which is the cookie that matches this one?

I spy with my little eye 3 tasty sandwiches.

And Dancer swooshed past on the slopes

Find 2 careening cats.

Find two pairs of yellow skis.

Slipperier than a silvery eel, someone's skiing on a banana peel.

and zoomed clear out of sight.

I spy with my little eye 10 frosty snowmen.

To protect against a mishap, who has a lucky feather tucked in their cap?

children's Christmas letters.

There's so many letters in here to go through. Can you find 5 with stamps that are blue?

I spy with my little eye the Holiday Mail Snail.

The only thing that could be better would be a twin to this cute sweater.

Find 6 pink mittens.

I spy a little fox who isn't having any fun. He's been knitting for so long, but his sweater's come undone.

Vixen helped the knitting club

The mice in the knitting room are running amok.
Where is the one napping in a hammock?

Why is this sweater unraveling?

make cozy Christmas sweaters.

Comet was at the ice rink,

Point out 3 peeking penguins.

This is quite a bugaboo; find 4 critters that start with W: a whale, worm, walrus, and wolf.

I spy with my little eye 3 things that rhyme with "ice": dice, mice, and an orange slice.

where winter sports are played.

They might be skating figure eights; find a pair of purple skates.

And Cupid popped by the factory

I spy with my little eye 7 tiny teddies each color of the rainbow.

Which of these rocking horses is unique?

Count 3 bottles of glue, 2 screwdrivers, and 1 saw, too.

to learn how toys are made.

Its tippy-tapping raises quite a clamor. Find a delightfully undersized hammer.

To find this one, you might have to look far. Find a big wooden block with one red star.

Donner was in the forest hanging lights

Pick out the pretty pickle.

This pink-petaled ornament must have been made by a florist. Can you find 2 more just like it in this forest?

and ornaments.

Find 4 a-peeling bananas.

I spy with my little eye 5 things that start with S: a sheep, slipper, spaghetti, scarf, and snake.

And Blitzen was getting wrapped up

Find the two tape dispensers that match.

These gifts are no surprise at all — can you find a wrapped bike, teddy bear, and ball?

with the last of the presents.

Can you count 8 red bows?

I spy with my little eye a penguin with a red bow tie.

Let's go! Hurry, everyone!

I spy with my little eye 5 snowy owls.

Time's almost up, but the reindeer are still carefree. Can you find the friends taking a selfie?

Twinkle, twinkle, little stars. Can you find where 10 are?

FLYING for Beginners

It's time to pull the sleigh!

Where is the missing jingle bell?

There are only 8 reindeer on the roster.
Which is the extra costumed imposter?

Just in time for take-off.
Merry Christmas!

Most gifts were packed in the sleigh, but some were not. Find 3 presents that Santa forgot.

I spy with my little eye 5 things that rhyme with "North Pole": a scroll, bowl, hole, mole, and a bag of coal.

Count 10 elves with yellow caps.

Now, on your way!

Spot 4 feathered friends in the crowd waving goodbye.

COAL

Answers

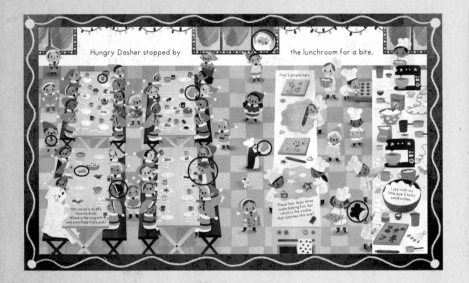